Rebecca Gugger and **Simon Röthlisberger** were both born in Switzerland and live together in Thun—near forests, mountains, and fresh air. Rebecca is a freelance illustrator and graphic designer, studied at the HKB (Bern University of the Arts), and likes to have her head in the clouds. Simon is a trained graphic designer currently working as an art director and has been known to hoist a sail or two. Every now and then the two work together as a team, wielding pen and pencil side by side.

Rebecca Gugger
Simon Röthlisberger

The
MOUNTAIN

Translated by Marshall Yarbrough

North
South

"The mountain
is a forest,
full of trees
and green things!"

claimed the bear.

"Not at all.
What are you thinking?
The mountain is a meadow.
There are flowers and herbs
and fresh smells
and the buzzing of bees,"

said the sheep.

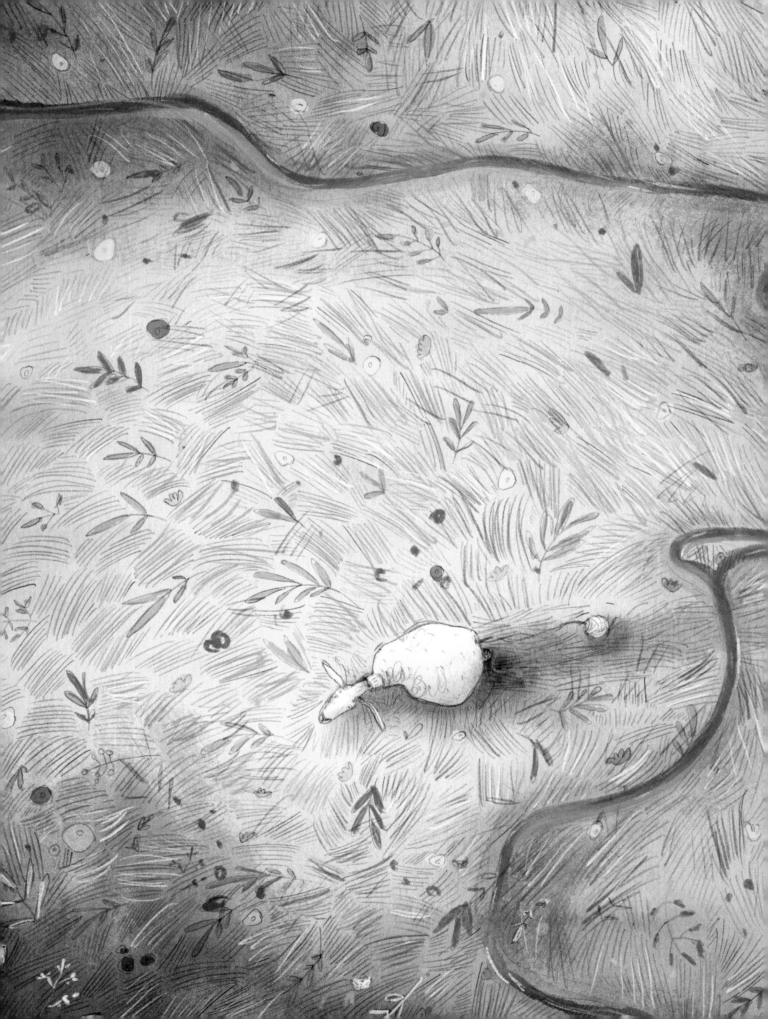

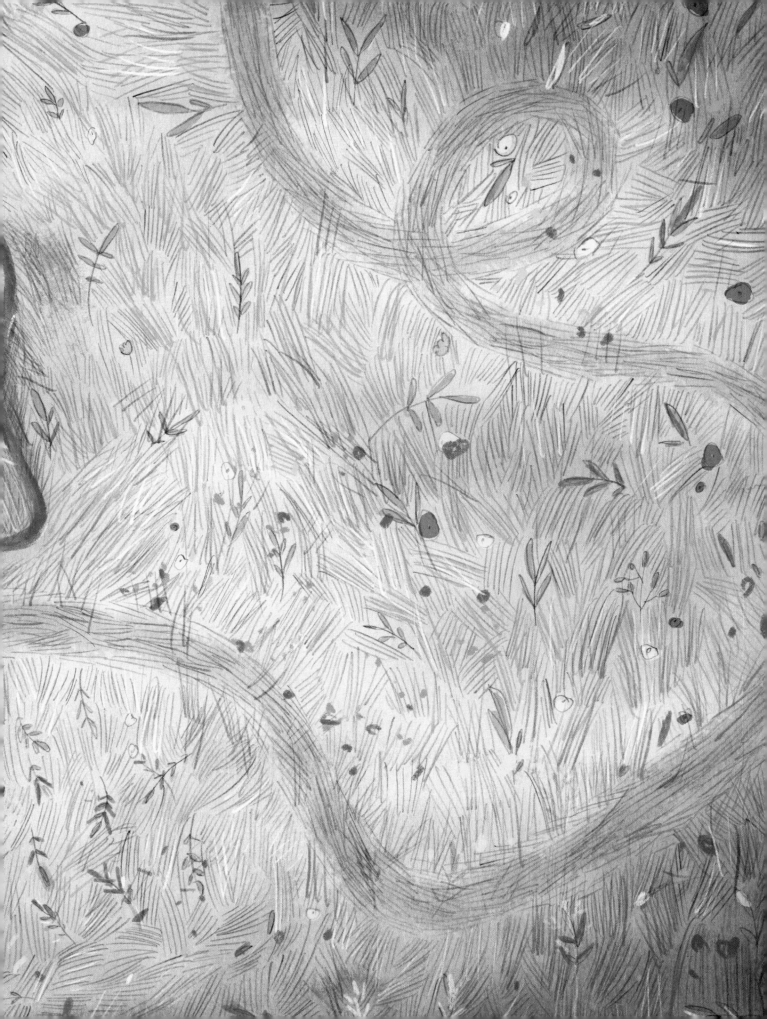

"You don't have a clue,
any of you!
The mountain is wet
and surrounded by water.
It's full of fish
and fine colors,"

blubbered the octopus.

"No way!
You're all a bunch of dopes.
We built the mountain!
It's dark and earthy
and like a maze
with lots of tunnels,"

said the ant, flexing its muscles.

"No!
The mountain is rocky
and stony and steep!"

cried the chamois, aghast.

"You and your
wild ideas.
White is what it is.
Up on the mountain
it's white everywhere.
And cold,"

said the snow hare.

The animals all shook their heads angrily.

"The others have no idea! They're all totally wrong!"

Soon everybody was shouting at everybody else.
But which one of them was right?

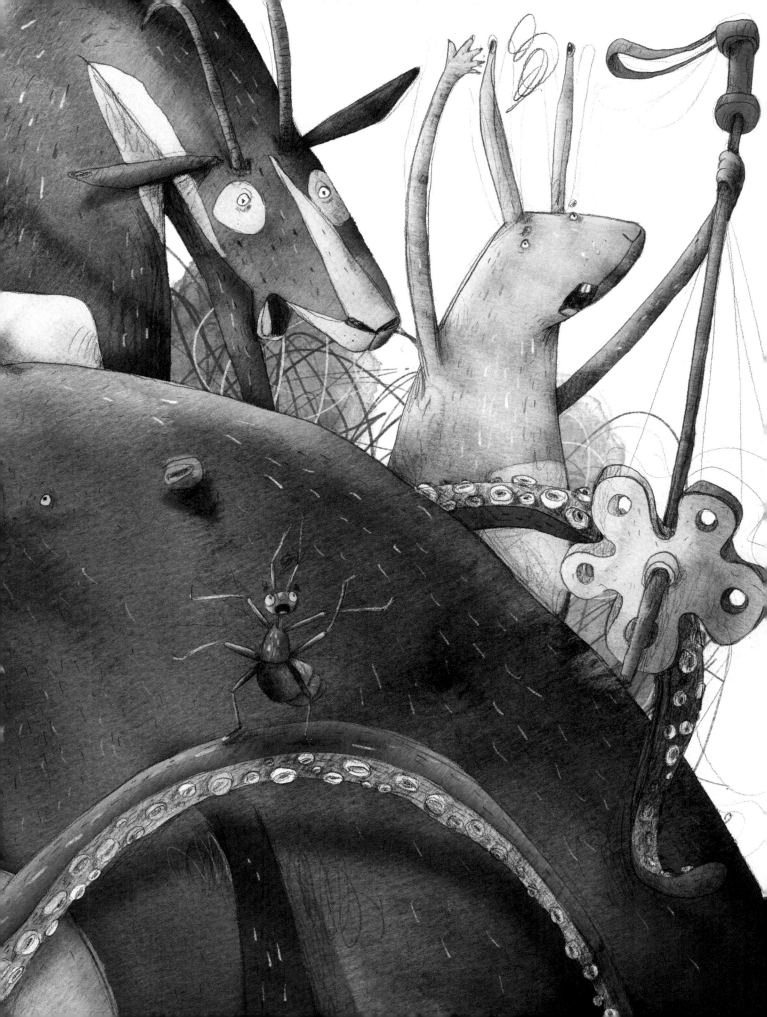

"Enough with this yelling.
I can't stand it anymore,"

thought the bird, and called out to the animals,

"How many of you
have ever actually
been up on the mountain?"

No one said a word.

"Do I dare?"

each animal thought to itself.

"Sure, I'll show everyone how right I am!"

Excitedly they all started climbing.

Curious, bold, fearful,
brave, fleet-footed, and high-spirited,
the animals set off on their way.

When they reached the top,
a big surprise awaited them.

Everything looked quite different.
Not like they'd expected.

Forest, meadow, rock and snow,
hills and water as far as
the eye could see.

Silently they sat together
and marveled. How small
everything looked from up here.

"Actually, it's quite simple,"

the animals said.